PO|

TO

PONDER

Robin Barton

Illustrated and compiled by Melissa Muldoon

ISBN - 9798377165590

Part I

Poems

to

Ponder

Tipping Point – *Almost a sonnet*

The morning stretches grey up to the moor,
Down the long valley lies a tongue of mist.
In alders, brambles, or in tamarisk,
Against the light, stencilled in sycamore

A linnet sweetly pricks the air with song.
From far across the bay the dawning grows,
Pines scent the air, an early golfer strolls,
A skylark trills, a jogger swings along,

Beside his path the black slugs slickly shine.
A stonechat chafes the air to warn his mate
A buzzard soars and yelps and sees a sign –
A beetle stirring, heedless of its fate.

But on this God-gift turf in harsh antithesis
Lie prams, beds, tires and trash: this is – a tipping point.

At the Wood's Edge

At the edge of the wood I sit in the sun,
Above me tall pines and thickets of thorn.
Below, a field slopes and shadows pass
As cloud and sunlight softly contend
When summer grips spring in a strong embrace.

Across the valley another wood
Where alder and larch and whitebeam stand,
Where wrens in ivy trill at their nests
Where once, sadly addled, some eggs we found
And the owl pierced the night with his ghostly cry.

With the wood at my back I am walled and secure,
For behind the wood is a sunken lane
And another wood and another field
And the quiet river silverly glides
And peace is the noontide blessing on all.

No quieter spot lives under the sun,
Though a rustle of winter leaves may stir,
While I turn my page or lift my gaze
To wonder at lives of smallest scope
The ant, the beetle, the bee in its flower,
The swallow, the moth or the tortoiseshell.

Yet here there are ghosts of darker days
And at the wood's corner, now smothered, scarce seen,
A rotting hut, broken and tangled with brier,
Within, a piano, worm-eaten and warped
But only harsh janglings you still might evoke:

For next to the hut, smashed and sunken in earth
A circle of steel and glass smithereens
Are all that remain of the thunder of war —
A searchlight's black skeleton, once a brave eye

To blazon an enemy high in the night;
And echoes of that time so distant, yet here,
A faint obbligato of fear-filled days
To counterpoint peace and these sun-filled hours,
And now only cloud shadows, passing like these.

Trespassing

Under the wire the mushrooms grew
White and thick
The size of tea plates.

I reached under the wire.

Before plucking
I saw a pair of leather boots
Well dubbined,
Thick, brown,
Built for the country,
Not boots to argue with.

Above the boots
Thick worsted socks,
Thick, brown.

Above the socks
Tweed trousers,
Thick, brown –
With a weave of green
And a weave of grey.
Beside the boots
Something straight and thick
At the top a hand
Knobbled and full of pain

Beside the hand
A waistcoat and watch.
Above the waistcoat
And the watch
A dark face hiding the sun.
Above the head
A hat
Thick, brown
With a weave of green
And a weave of grey.

Out of the face a voice
The colour of coal
Catechising.
'The commandments, boy – number eight?'
The head was black against the sun
'Number eight, boy!'

Ashamed, my hand drew back.
The mushrooms, unplucked,
Perfect tea plate size
Deliciously
Grew on.

Remote Control

(A day in Waziristan)*

Like a double cross
It doubles across the sky
Unseen it flies —
Such intricacies!

Decades of cunning thought
Compressed in laminates of Kevlar,
Wood and aluminium
Carbon and quartz —
It's rocket science.

*   *

Like a squirming ball
On earth a baby crawls
Seen by all eyes —
Such intricacies!

Decades of hope and love
Compressed in laminates of
Flesh and blood and bone
Breath and birth —
It's father-mother science.

*   *

Here is the drone called Predator.
Along its wings titanium edged
Minutest pores allow
Weeping holes. Through these
Seep molecules of glycol
That no ice should hinder

Progress.

Here is the crone called Aaminah.
Within her voice, grief razor edged,
Illimitable pain.
Across her arms she bears
Daughter and child
For whom no heart could calculate

Such loss.

*Based on extensive research, the Bureau of Investigative
Journalism found that between 391 – 780 civilians were killed out of a
total of between 1,658 and 2,597 and that 160 children are reported
among the deaths.*

Small Change

Darwin upon Galapagos
Saw little birds and did not guess
What would their little beaks evolve.
So small the changes. But how far
Across the worlds of thought and life
They pecked and pecked into his brain
And ushered in such angry strife.

Darwin upon Galapagos
Shot little finches, as he thought,
(For now they fit a different race)
Each had a beak of varied size
But knew not how so small a change
Selected for each natural need
Led some to say 'Darwin's deranged'.

Darwin left Galapagos
Without a thought about the birds
Until an ornithologist
Declared, 'How like they are to those
Still found in Chile though they live
A thousand leagues beyond her shores
Amid a barren waste of sea.'

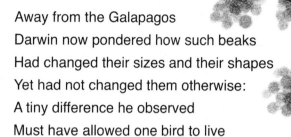

Away from the Galapagos
Darwin now pondered how such beaks
Had changed their sizes and their shapes
Yet had not changed them otherwise:
A tiny difference he observed
Must have allowed one bird to live
A fuller life and so reserved

Him of the subtler beak to dwell
A little longer and more well.
Thus piece by piece the theory grew
How tiny changes newly shaped
(Whenever an advantage came)
The species, so that, through long years,
A newer creature came to be.

Darwin upon Galapagos
From such unbidden processes
Analogised, analogised
Till men from monkeys, he announced,
(Though I have told the simpler tale)
And cries and accusations came,
'Blasphemer, antichrist and devil!'

The world all Biblically armed
Declared such theories warred with God
And in His battle lines they fought
Or thought they fought, for He above
Remained insouciant, unmoved,
And did not seem to take command.
Perhaps He sent the thought abroad:

'Let those who best selected are
Survive most fitted to divine the truth.

Levellers Day:
Burford Church May 17th 1649

There is blood on the grass and stones
More blood near the ancient bones
A whiff of sulphurous smoke
Three white clouds that drift to the oak.

Each soldier droops dead from his stake
Where primroses smile at daybreak.
The churchyard thrushes have ceased.
In the church are more unreleased –

Three hundred who hammer the door.
Three levellers lie by the wall
Thomson and Perkins alone
With Church by the grey gravestone.

They bayed for the moon long ago
Free votes, free religion, fair law
Till Cromwellian guns said 'No!'
But they'd chiselled a crack in the door.

Disguises

Out on the sea white triangles,
Mere pictures on a calm expanse.
Distance removes whatever life
Could be unveiled by nearer view.

An old man's gnarled and rheumy face.
Saddens the street he rides along
But years ago he changed the world
With courage in war's crucible.

Upon an arid desert floor
Where fires have left black-silvered ash
With bark-like black-leaved deadly skin
A lizard, glue-tongued, swallows ants.

A tiger burns in dappled light:
All unaware a fawn might dream
Of mother's milk, until a paw
Or nightmare fang secures its end.

A squalid caterpillar squirms
Or with snake eyes repels its foes
But sheds its skin and wakens wings
To dazzle peacocks' gaudy fans.

Do all things wear a lying mask
And hide within a secret sin –
Or triumph – that the world knows not,
Or nurture beauty with disguise?

Mediterranean Sport

At dawn the hunters move through woodland trails.
Bravely in khaki coats they lurch along,
Their rifles boldly point the seaward way.
In heather hollows soon they nestle down,
Drink coffee, wine, eat caponata pies
And wait while light grows deadlier with the day.

Far in the south the sea is misty slate;
Above, the sky's a sly blue killing ground.
The hunters, hundreds strong, behold their prey:
Who wounds a swift or swallow's counted best –
As marksman of superior sightedness.
Or who kills rarest falcon, dove or finch
Exults in pride, honoured by man and boy,
That pits his steel against the soft-downed breasts
Of swift or martin, wryneck, nightjar, lark.
All fall in thousands, fluttering in the throes
The hopeless death throes, gifts of finest sport.

The men, well cheered, sit for their photographs
Showing their teeth and dying prey with pride.
The day has started well, though someone says:
'Five years ago the skies were darker far,
The flocks more dense the species more diverse.
Another five and we'll no longer need
A use for guns: the skies will say, "All Clear!" –
Our aims accomplished, our rewards received.'

Trapped

Within dim misted lights and giant trees,
Within intimidating heat, breathless humidity,
The fatal exudations sweat down trunks
Riven by gnarled old age, a billion years ago.

Around some smooth alluring necks today
We see the golden moments time has wrought
When, resting fatally, some fly or moth,
Some busy ant, some mantis, wasp or bug
Some millipede or nectar laden bee,
With but a careless touch was mired and trapped
And knew its slow inevitable fate.

Like lava creeping and enveloping
Stifling all efforts, feeble helplessness,
The amber from the ancient pine crept down
And drowned its victims hour by silent hour
That now the creatures' direst agonies
As cruel gifts of time adorn and charm.

Buzzard

'... Food: Mice, rats, moles and young rabbits, reptiles, beetles, carrion and worms'

Edmund Sandars: *'A Bird Book for the Pocket'*

In rings it soars with moor and marsh below,
      Close to the clouds, a shape of fear to fauna
Far beneath. In gullies, brakes and briars,
      In hollows, rocky dens and gorse strewn fells
Mouse, mole, young rabbit, rat and vole beware
      The circling menace, stiffen, if aware,
Fearing the silent drop, the taloned grip,
      The squeezing death, the rip of a hooked beak.

Yet lesser breeds, the beetle, bug, and worm,
      Know nothing, nothing fear beneath that sky
But, equal-fated, meet an equal fate,
      Ignobler victims, but unsuffering.

I try to see connection: knowing less
      Is it a blessing not to know our fate
Thereby to fear it less? Or is to know,
      And therefore fear what it will be,
Our armour to extend fulfilment, life
      Or hope? Or is the very fear of ends
A false fear to be tattered by a truth
      That true life is not matter-bound to earth?

The buzzard soars. Its poise upon the wind
     Is greater than its fall upon the earth.
If thought soars, let it stay the winds
     Of fear. And let it never drop to feed
On carrion dread but balance on winged mind.

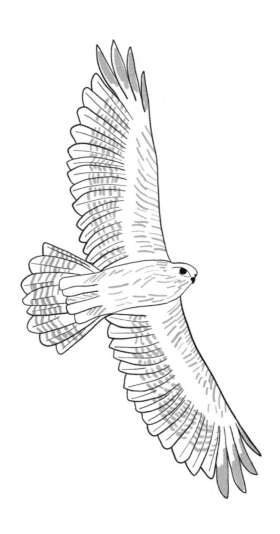

Faded Velvet

You wanted your velvet-covered riding helmet restored
Every earthly thing fades and loses gloss.
You are asking for creation to start over again –
But better – no fading or dying possible.

God, if he'd thought a bit longer, instead of trying to get
                    everything done in less than a week
Could have used an hour or so of day seven
To put in some fixer, like a photographer
Developing his photograph so the image wouldn't fade.

Of course a mere mortal photographer
Can't do that – the photo will still fade unless you hide it in
                    the dark.
But surely God could have done it?
Wasn't there something complacent when he looked at
                    everything
And said to himself, 'This is really very good!'?

Perhaps, though, being entirely Spirit,
He could only make spiritual stuff – like a photographer,
                    yes, in a way –
A maker of images.

Now if we were to be just images – spiritual stuff,
Images in the old fellow's mind,
We wouldn't fade, we wouldn't even go wrong in any sense

Moon 1969

Old Lady.
You finally lost your virginity.
The rocket, sperm-like,
Sank home.

Now, with the night your womb,
To what children will you
Give birth?

Mutation

Singularity: ... a point in space-time at which matter is compressed to an infinitely great density (Chambers).

From singularity to singularity
What lies between? The Big Bang, we are told,
Some billion years ago. And after billions more
The Big Implosion comes till all that is
Into a single point is squeezed.

And in between some spark, it seems,
Emerged as life — destined to die.

From atom to diatom, cell on cell,
From the primeval soup, from unknown source
The germ of life developed, change on change,
Darwin decreed, but could not say from where.

And more than bodies infinitely small
And more than bodies larger and diverse
Some power accumulated sense on sense
And at the climax consciousness arose
No man knows how.

The sun shines forth a trillion trillion rays
And every ray its parent image bears
As warmth and light and beauty, nothing dark.
Oceans contain some trillion trillion drops
And every drop its parent nature bears,
As freshness, nutriment and stimulus.

So from some source of infinite design
Some source of wisdom, infinitely good
Might come reflections, infinite, diverse,
To image that great goodness, perfect, whole.
And those bright images be both you and me
Mutating from the matter universe
Escaping cycles of all space and time
Into the paradise long lost to sight,
Into Nirvana, to that state of mind
Wherein is only love's unending peace.

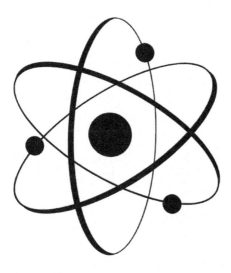

Distance

(The Solent, from Pennington Marshes, September 2008)

This is a universe of calm horizons and of nothing harsh.
This is a region of untroubled life.
Along the shore movements are small and secret.
Bird cries are faint and distant and the sea's asleep.
Under weed and boulder only the thought of life informs us
                                                            there is life.

Reflections breed reflections, sky on sea,
Soft-blooming cloud illuming lakes of light.
Far, far upon the mirror of the sea there is no stir of air
To move the distant sails, mere points of white.
Content with lowness, island and mainland lie
At rest upon the Solent's still embrace,
And distance is the soul of this hour's peace,
Of this time's place.

Overheard

I lie at rest in winter's vale
And hear the world and see its frown
The storm clouds gather black and wild -
Death at the door is calling all,
Tyrants and slaves ferment the earth,
Satanic liars tell their lies -
The ghosts of war, the shades of fear;
Corruption's coin fills men's hands
Diseases' whispers fill the air,
Gunmen fire ignorance's shots
And hatred belches from the earth.

And yet across this self-same Earth
Some shafts of truth unveil its ills,
Time's spade forever turns its sods
And all its tares come clear to burn.
The heart knows errors have no truth
And without truth no lie is real.
Trees stand as preachers to the soul:
The acorn, love, towers over all.

Rebel

99.999999999999 % of an atom's volume is just empty space!*

A block of stone two metres cubed
Is really so much empty space.
Each tiny atom's only truth
Is so infinitesimally small
It is out-voted by the space
That fills the walls it sits inside.
Out-numbered by a ratio
Of more than ninety ninety-nines
Times greater than its tiny self.

There is a rebel thought which says
'What if this void is telling us
That only thought maintains the notion
That what is seen is what is real
And that this notion's mere belief.
And this earth's life and what we see
Is really but the mind's belief -
We only see what we believe
And only feel what we believe
And that belief alone is all
That keeps us thralled to limits old:
What the world *thinks* is what seems true.'

Placebos often have effect
Because, it seems, we think we're cured
Though only sugar, free of drug,
Is all the little pill contained.

So if all thought were different
And thus changed what belief thought true
What a rebellion would ensue -
And Change - for better or for worse -
This wild globe of swirling thought
Into new chaos - or else bring
The true Shekinah to our view.

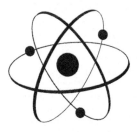

If we drew an atom and made protons and neutrons a centimetre in diameter, then the electrons and quarks would be less than the diameter of a hair and the entire atom's diameter would be about ten kilometers across. - from the Lawrence Berkeley National Laboratory web site.

'There is nothing either good or bad, but thinking makes it so.' (Shakespeare)

Kaleidoscope

Cleopatra, said the Stratford bard,
was exemplar of infinity
In terms of female volatility
Variety of humour, beauty, wrath,
Ill-temper, kindliness and love.
Approach her with a flattering, unctious word
She would seem pleased but keep reserved
The possibility that if one erred
In keeping pace with every changing mood,
Her temper flared, her eye shot barbs of steel,
Her sharp command would swiftly order whips
Unjustly wielded upon angel flesh.

Yet to her maids she rendered amity
Such as drew tears from them and soft-breathed praise
And at her death such loyalty and grace
That the mere thought of hers brought death itself
To one - no outward cause but only this:
Pure grief, Iras thus died, and Charmain,
Fearless in love, as Cleopatra slept, she too
Seized the vile asp and, as her mistress, died.

See in a single case, a single character
Exemplar of variety; then think of all
And we touch but an atom of infinity;
Think but of flowers, faces, birds or skies,
Music's great concords, voices, cadences,
The fallen brave, the lives to come, the stars,
Chameleon changes in the season's hues
And with Blake's image of a grain of sand
We see infinity's kaleidoscope.

Chimes at Midnight

(See Henry IV Part 2:III.ii)

'We have heard the chimes at midnight, Master Shallow,'
Old Falstaff speaking, young long years ago.
Yes, Falstaff speaking, more improbable a man
For fighting no man reckons reckoning his girth.
A sad man thinking youth and strength still there
Though long left on the bloody fields of war
And in the Boar's Head tavern, in Eastcheap.
Yet, still a hero, ready for new birth,
New fields, new strategems new honours bright -
So self-decieved, a schoolboy braying lies.

He's on recruit to prick six men to fight
Their names a register of feebleness and age;
Ralph Mould, Shadow, Thomas Wart
Next Feeble, Peter Bull-Calf of the Green
Pricked on the list protesting a disease,
Two other non men, lacking even names -
The task is done, a dotage of grey men
Is called to arms. Now to the tavern's rife
With cuckolding and spirits and good cheer
Old Falstaff blots out actuality.

And so it is the old know death is near
And some would duel the dying of the light
And some would reach the doorway with light step
And some laugh and jeer the midnight path
To reach a land that few have walked again.
Perhaps there's no more to it but a dream
Of walking to old paths, old days, not new;
Of passing through an arch with no more thought
But that the dream before was just the same.

Part II

Bible

Raps

and

Rhymes

The Forfeit

In Eden long ago, a tale is told,
Of purling streams and wonders manifold
And in this garden, all refreshed the mind,
Where Adam (first, supposed, of human kind)
Wandered unlabouring with Eve his wife,
A paradise of love where never strife
Was heard nor evil, storm nor stress occurred
But joyful sounds of fountain, zephyr, bird.
Soft breezes fanned the glades and stars shone clear
Through balmy nights; where never fear
Of any kind could ever lodgement find
Nor creature hid from hunter, stag nor hind.

Perhaps who told this tale could not but sow
Some darkling seed of fate, and cause to grow
Like smallest cloud springing from purest blue
That swiftly darkens all the land to brew
Thunder and travail, lightnings, fire and fume
That from the purest light spreads blackening gloom,
Envious, perhaps, that earth should breed perfection
Who in his life had known only rejection.

There were two trees, the one gave life and love,
The other, more exotic, from above —
Or so said one — had fruit of such allure
As filled the mind with thousand thoughts impure.
Such was this earthly defect guised as fruit
Whose deadly beauty in Eve's heart took root.
She knew there lurked within a hidden power
Beneath its rind, swollen from out its flower —
She knew. And so she passed each day this tree
And smiled knowing such wrong could never be
Smallest temptation; for her inward voice
(Some say of God), told her that such a choice
Would bring disaster, death, decay and woe,
Would bring into the world a deadly foe.

But on a day, coiling upon a bough
A serpent inched its length and pondered how
To tempt the pair of lovers, from their pride,
As he in envy watched them, side by side
In gentle talk and whispered lovers' vows
Such as sweet nature youthful love allows.

Now, you will say, "Your tale is quite absurd:
A thinking serpent, no more than a bird
Can calculate its actions, think or plan…"
But wait, for as Eve passed he then began —
(You'll not believe this) — he began to *speak*.

'O Eve,' he said, (at which her knees turned weak)
'I hear that tree you pass bears special fruit.
But that some rumour says it would not suit.
To eat it. If you did, so runs the tale,
You'd die. This story's a deceitful veil
Hiding the truth that, far from death, you'd see
As God sees, and you'd have true wisdom's key
And true discernment, knowing good from bad,
A fruit to end all woes and make men glad.'

His words struck home. For long her mind had thought
How strange it was no other fruit she sought
Had ever been forbidden, nor no tree
Bore fruit that to their tasting was not free
Save this. Now, more than all, this drew her on
To contemplate his words and think upon
The wisdom and the knowledge that they meant.
And as she stood a gentle breeze fanned scent
Intoxicating from the tree and from the flesh
Of this fair fruit, so beautiful, so fresh.
It magnified itself before her eyes
As food nutritious and to make one wise.

And so she stretched her arm, so lithe and strong
To pluck the fruit, suppressing thoughts of wrong
And bit into its fatal, damning flesh
And with that single bite into the mesh
Of evil's subtle net all men ensnared.
And evilly since then, all men have fared.

And Adam, passing nearby, in a dream,
Unthinkingly, since Eve could never seem
Or, still less, be less than his perfect love,
Took of the selfsame fruit; till one above
At evening sought them and with ominous voice
And solemn, learning their fatal choice,
Condemned them evermore to roam the earth,
Till only through repentance and new birth
Tilling the soil of error with remorse
They paid the forfeit of that deadly course.

Envoi

Now at this story do not take offence:
It is not history nor literal truth.
The key is: there has never been
A talking snake. This fact makes clear
That this old tale is allegorical:
The snake tells lies but they are meant to show
That all its words are lies we must unmask.
For truth we need remember those first words
Describing man as in God's image made.
This was the man God made, complete and good.
Adam, the dreamer, was a counterfeit.
Think on the first man, hold to him and her.

The Sore Loser

Yo've heard of Adam yo've heard of Eve
Now I'll tell yo nuther story y'all not believe.
Well nobody believe it, nobody a-tall
'Cos of what de old Bible tell 'bout de so-called 'Fall,'
Cos de Bible tell 'bout a talkin' snake —
Aint never bin such a crittur so de Bible's fake.

Now a aint sayin' eva word be true
Least not in the way youse tink blue be blue,
'Cos youse godda unnerstan' taint de lidderal truth
But de truth at de heart gives y'all de proof:
What de spirrit unnerstan' neath' de lidderal word
Give y'all ways t' go in dis troublesome world.

Still, aint nobody b'lieve de Bible no more
N'iff ya mention de word they say yo a bore.

But hear yo a story don't sound so dumb
'Bout wickedness 'n' evil till kingdom come
'Bout a fella name Abel and sweet brother Cain —
Them's a template for all how t' cause bitter pain.

Now dis Cain was a farmer, spent all days sweatin' plough
No tractor them days, just de sweata his brow.
Come the harvest he rakes up a few bundles 've rye
Reckons God'll be made when they fall neath his eye.

Sets 'em up on some altar – jest a slab on some stones
Didn' take that much trouble – a was worn to's bones.
Lights up all dese bundles to set up de smoke,
Thinks, 'God'll like it like weed, like us ornery folk.'

But then brother Abel, a shepherd by trade,
'Sides ta make God an offrin' 've much higher grade
Not, lemme say, cos he wanna make trouble,
Prob'ly didn' even know 'bout Cain's rye stubble,
Just nat'ral goodness made him pick his best lamb
Thinkin,' 'Gotta give God the best that A can.'
And that was the best and the lamb's best cuts
He set on his altar (made sweatin' his guts —
Eva' stone cut square so it fitted just right).
An' de sweet smell 've lamb roasted long that night
Rose up ta God's nostrils till He breathed the aroma
And thoughta Hisself, 'A must give de diploma
Between these two brothers ta young brother Abel,
He's taken more trouble ta lay on his table
Something 'a valued much more than fren' Cain
Whose offrin' was routine, done with disdain:
Some moth-eaten sheaves of half ripened rye?
Yo'd never think once to make pastry or pie'

So God came and chatted to Abel and said,
'Well done, lad, well done lad. Come an' have dinna.
Wi' a bit a mint sauce youse cookin'' s a winna.'

Now Cain, jus' in hearin', grew red in de face.
Yow'd think he'd been runnin' ta win a big race.
A scowled and muttered, bit his lip till it bled.
God notice and warn him, 'Recall what A said?
Some sin lies crouchin' to spring inta ya mine
Like a tiger so eager to kill what it fine.
Yo muss cage such a' animal, seal its fate
Less yo come to a' end 'cos of all yo' hate.'
But nex marnin' Cain rose up an' said to his bro —
Pretendin' all frienly zif he warn't no foe —
'Bro Abel ma fren', less tek a nice walk,
Less go in de country an' have a nice talk.'

Poor Abel, still thinkin' how God 'a bin kind'
Said 'Gladly, old fella, what have yo in mine?'
'See this rock?' now sez Cain, 'Come closer and look.'
And swift as a snake wid de rock he took
But a second to kill his own brother stone dead.

Now it didn't take long his deed came to de head
'A de Lord above (though it might ha' bin better
If Him up in heaven ta stop de vendetta
Had warned friend Abel 've Cain's intent
An' tole him true what de walkin' meant).
But ta Cain he said, 'Where is Abel yo brother?'
But Cain repla', 'What? Am a's keeper?
'Spect at this hour a dey ya'll fine him a sleeper.
Look aroun'. Doan yo know? With yo'all seein' eye?
An' yo' talk of dinna an' lamb an' mince pie?'

So de Lord, He angry, say, 'What sin ha' yo done?
What horror on eart' have yo don' to ma son?
Doan yo hear fra de groun' Abel's blood cryin loud?
It's a-callin' revenge reachin' high ta de cloud'
Yo muss run from dis lan' and wander tha earth'
'Cos it woan any longer grow crop, but a dearth
Will come with the curse a' now say. So go,
Yo a' enemy now, ta all men a foe:
Go wander and roam in the land of Nod.'

But Cain cried in dread for his life unta God
'This sentence is horror, dey will cut off ma head
Fa'f anyone see me – he kill me stone dead.'
But God, knowin' the law, sez, 'There'll be no more strife
For seven more die in revenge for yo' life –
No, 'stead, A'll burn on yo' face dis bran'
So 'f any one see yo he'll know he can
Never dispose a yo, pain o' death,
He'll know yo' a'cursed till yo' dyin' breath!'

So Cain, sore loser 'tween Abel an' him,
Left his lan' an' fiels ta 'tone fo' his sin.
An' ever sin' then yo will hear this proverb:
'The mark a Cain' means, "Cursed ba God's word"'

Flood

About five thousand years ago,
Old Noah, so the Bible says,
Was told by God to build an ark,
A ship to house, by twos and twos,
All creatures, male and female kinds.
And not the least were Mrs Noah
With their three sons, Ham, Shem and Japheth
Who with their wives some eight in all,
Humans, that is, as we are told,
Must cruise in safety while the flood
Raged on the earth when God grew vexed.

Now here's a thing that puzzles me:
'In just a week,' said good old God,
'You, Noah, must now gather these
And lodge them safely in the ark.'

Did Noah then protest or not?
Did he not think, 'That really isn't
A skill I have. Why t'other day
A good old cockerel I tried
To gather up for Mrs Noah
To make a nice roast, just for two.
The bird had done his service well
All that begetting and begetting
Had swelled our chicken run just fine.
But, wily bird, he flapped and scurried,

It took best part of half an hour
For me to grab him, tie his legs
Then fetch the axe to lop his head.
And Mrs Noah laughed aloud
To see my old limbs dash around
And raise the dust about the yard.
So how you think, Dear God, that I,
Six hundred years of age, mark you,
In just a matter of a week
Can carry out this quaint request —
Or rather order — your behest
To fill with earth's menagerie
This little ship, or rather, boat —
I'm sorry, but it just won't do,
The task's too big a job for me,

It's far too short, the time allowed,
Just do the maths, and you'll soon see
In one day, four and twenty hours, —
No resting, mind, no breaks for tea —
At that rate I would only catch
Just forty-eight of all you want.
And in a week of non-stop toil
Three hundred and but fifty-six
Out of, say fifty million more,
Would scarcely scratch, as you may see,
The surface of Your Grace's task.
And what about – excuse my words –
The matter of the food supplies?

Are we to feed upon our stores
Of creatures we must bring aboard?
I thought the whole point was to save
The planet's livestock, not reduce
Each precious species to a rump
Of those survivors of this flood
Which, in your wisdom, you will cause.

Biodiversity, I see,
Is not perhaps what you intend
Though it may seem to be your plan.

And even if by wondrous means
I caught the fifty million beasts
That wander earth from seas to peaks
How do you think they'd all squeeze in?
The ark is only but the length
(And a bit more) of a football pitch.'

By words like these old Noah could
Have set God wise and stood his ground.

And here's another thing: just think,
If poor old Noah had to gather
A pair of every living thing
Wouldn't that mean he'd have to go
To every corner of the earth?
Did he have wings and could he fly
Beyond mach 5 and back again

Each time he managed to ensnare
A lucky pair of ants or bears?
It's true he'd only need one slug
Or one snail in its little house
Because, as no doubt you will know,
These need no mates to do the job
Of reproduction – all alone
Hermaphroditicly they bear
Some thousands that their image wear.
And thus for Noah they'd reduce
His labours by a sec or two.

But I digress. Why press the point?
The thing's impossible, I think.
It surely must be just a fable
Or, to be fair, a nice par-able
That thus, as Shakespeare might have said,
'By indirections to find out
Directions', that is, Truth, and so
Suggests that if you do your best
God will support you, give you rest.

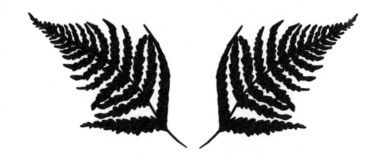

Written in Stone

High on Mount Sinai Moses stood
Bravely he faced Almighty God
Who said, 'My friend, now if you would,
     – and please don't think that this is odd –

Take down these blocks of solid stone
Whereon I've written laws for all
To keep. And see they do not groan
When in amongst them is the call

To treat me as their only God
Though they'd prefer a golden calf.
A calf a god! By Aaron's rod
I swear, it almost makes me laugh.

For while we've had a jolly time
Here on mount Sinai and you've seen
The wisdom of these laws sublime
Your folk down there are all too keen

To make their own god out of gold
Aaron, alas, was much too weak
To stop them as they made the mould
For all the gold he'd bade them seek

From wives and daughters all gold bling
And melted down each shiny jewel
As everyone danced round to sing
Songs painting you dear friend a fool

Or that you'd disappeared up here
And left them there to stew in heat
While leaving them a prey to fear
All leaderless and nowt to eat.'

So Moses grabbed the precious tables
And soon descended in a bate
To see that God had told no fables:
There stood the calf: he was too late

He saw them dance and jig and sing
And (much much worse) in naked pairs
They slithered round O, dreadful thing,
As uninhibited as bears.

Poor Moses stood aghast and cross
He hurled the tablets from his grasp
And smashed them as if so much dross
To see him would have made you gasp.

And God Himself was not best pleased
And told old Moses he would kill
The lot of them and so be eased
Of His great anger, have His fill.

But bravely Moses calmed Him down
And said, 'But it was you, my Lord,
Who led these very folk from town
And made the Red Sea but a ford.

And it was you who promised us
You'd bring us to a new homeland.
So please, my Lord, make no more fuss
I'll be the surety for your commands,'

I'll melt that gold calf down and crush it
And water it to make a drink
For all the Israelites to flush it
Through their own bodies, make them think.

'Well, then,' said God, 'Carve out two more
Just two more tablets and return,
And with my finger I'll re-score
Commandments Ten for all to learn.'

Thus were the laws of God redone
And God for evermore has said:
'Follow them and, by my Son,
To health and happiness you'll be led.'

In the Den

What must have been his mien then
When Daniel, cast into the den,
Gazed where a square of stone let in
A ghost of light to light his sin?

And what could such beasts lying there
Discern of him now in their lair?
Could these imprisoned lions know
Or see in sombre gloom below

The face of innocence? or divine
An evil set to undermine
This man who soared above his foes,
An eagle over wrangling crows?

Or could they know the trumped up laws
That, once defied, led to their jaws?
And, knowing, they but lifted heads
And settled to their stony beds?

This Daniel, who, so wise and meek
So faithful, so intent to seek
Best policies his King might make
His foes had plotted now to break.

'O King,' they said, 'O King Darius!
This Jew, this Daniel is so pious,
That he, despite your new penned laws,
Prays thrice a day and does not pause

To make a loyal obeisance
To you, O King, but, in a trance
He at his window prays his Lord,
His God, thrice daily; is not awed

By our unbreakable injunction
But prays his god without compunction.'
Darius, trapped by his own law
Reluctantly sent to the door

Of that foul den his favoured friend.
Distraught, unable to amend
The cruel law, he fasted, wept,
Until at dawn he swiftly crept

Down to the den in hope to find
That Daniel, he of steadfast mind,
Could, 'gainst all odds be still alive
And by a wonder to've survived.

'O Daniel,' desperately he called,
'Has your god held the beasts in thrall
And hid you in his shielding arms,
And held you safely from all harms?'

And Daniel, unscathed, untorn
By tooth or claw or savage law
Cried to the king, 'By God's great grace
His angel stood before my face

And closed the jaws up of these beasts
So that we slumbered here in peace.'
The king in joy embraced his friend.
'I swear by your god I'll amend

The wicked law that led us here,
I'll hoist those devils insincere,
That played us false, by their decree.
They and their families then will see

That hatred of the just is sin.'
So those advisers and their kin
Suffered the very fate devised
For Daniel. And, the law revised,

A new decree was now proclaimed
Throughout the land, and God was named
The only God in whom to rest —
Assuredly all would be blessed.

The Burning Fiery Furnace

That pride and power go hand in hand
Now see how true: in a far-off land:
There on a plain for all to admire
Stood a golden plinth and a golden spire
'Bove a statue high and in letters of gold
Round the golden base was his story told:
An almighty king (with a name as long
As befits the King of Babylon).
"A great king's son and a conqueror
Nebuchadnezzar, Emperor."

Whenever upon the wings of the wind
The sound of the sackbut, lyre, woodwind,
The blare of the trumpet, oboe and drum
Bagpipe or zither or psaltery's thrum,
Should call like a summons in each subject's ears,
That – such were the megalomaniac's fears
(Encouraged by councillors with an agenda
To trap any Jew who might be an offender) —
Every man must then bow his head
And worship his king, his new godhead.

This petty demand, should one ignore,
Would now incur the wrath of law:
By cunning these councillors made the king swear
That any who failed to obey or might dare
To worship their own god and flout the king's charge

Must be thrown in the midst of a fire, supercharged,
A furnace so hot as to vaporise all
Who dared to refuse the cacophonous call
Of the blare of the trumpet, oboe and drum
Bagpipe or zither or psaltery's thrum.

And bow to the statue so tall and grand.
On hearing then that raucous band
Were three young Jews who would not dance
Or ever bow in obeisance
To the tune of terror the councillors played;
For the only law that they obeyed
Was God's alone. Their names I'll show:
Shadrach, Meshach, Abednego
So true so faithful, trusting, brave
No fear of death could them enslave.

The courtiers now rubbed hands in glee:
The Jewish lads, as all could see,
Had disobeyed their sovereign's law
And so the fire and furnace door
Would be their end. No more their power
Benignly rendered, brought to flower
In Babylon's behalf, would rule.
For they had been the kingdom's tool
To root out tyranny and crime
And work for justice in their time.

And now instead this racist clique
Could rule unchecked and keenly seek
To trap the king by his own law
And open wide the furnace door
To swallow up the exiles three.
And with their deaths to then be free.
Thus in the king's ear they announce
Their disobedience and denounce
Shadrach, Meshach Abednego
Into the furnace they must go.

Nebuchadnezzar, Nebuchadnezzar
Babylon's king at the end of his tether
Said, 'What did you say? What did you say?'
When all in a bother in court, that day,
His councillors, seething and filled with hate,
Saw how to seal their enemies' fate.
'Your statue O king, they would not salute,
To your statue, Lord, they cocked a snook.'
The king in a fury, shouted loud:
'What? To my statue have they not bowed?

'Open the furnace doors full wide
Heat it to seven times higher,' he cried,
'Thrust them full clothed now into the fire!'
The soldiers obeyed but then expired –
The heat had turned them all to ash
Their armour melted in a flash.
But Shadrach, Meshach Abednego

Stepped into the flames and it was so
That all at ease they walked and spoke
Unharmed midst the searing flames and smoke. –

Till Nebuchadnezzar arose amazed
As into the furnace he gazed and gazed.
'Do you not see?' he cried to his court,
'Those three young men just walk and talk!
And, tell me, tell me can it be true?
There's another man with them, someone new,
A man with the looks of the Son of God
But never so wonderful, strange or odd
Their clothes unscorched themselves quite well
With never a cinder or fiery smell!'

So at once King Nebuchadnezzar declared,
'If any man now should forbid the prayer
Of those who honour this race's gods
He needs must face the most fearsome odds
When he, being torn each limb from limb,
Seeks some other angel to rescue him.
For no other god but the god of the Jews
Can rescue, from whatever fate we choose,
A man who trusts the power of the Lord
To save him, whatever may evil accord.'

Jephthah

Now a'll tell ya a tale of sheer foolishness
How some folks, through pride, greed or jus' lucklessness
Make deals with God or the devil or who
And end losin' summat too precious ta lose.
Take Jephtha, a judge in them distant times.
It say 'judge' in de Bible, but in faraway climes
More a warlord than judge as what follows'll prove.
Hear the tragic event – you'll surely be moved.

'A was born out of wedlock, some harlot his mother,
So all cos of this 'a was shunned by's brothers
And sent to a land that the Bible calls Tob.
Soon he came head of a gang, did some jobs
So the word spread aroun' he was good in a fight
Now his half brothers facing some Ammonites
That held grudges cos of some trespassin' past,
Turned beggars to Jephtha, changing tunes real fast
They wanted his fightin' to fix up their mess.
'So ya want me now cos of Ammonite pests,
Said Jephtha, 'Well, see now, what can yous offa?'
They said, 'We'll make ya king an' all of our coffers
'll be yours to keep if ya'll kick out these dudes
These Ammonite heathens put an end ta these feuds.'

This Jephtha thought, 'Well, now here's a bargain.
'King ain't a bad deal, niff ah don' make a farthin''

So to seal this deal he swore to the Lord:
'If Ah knock out these Ammonites with yo' holy sword
Why, Dude, be ma pleasure to pay you whatever
Steps first from ma door after all this endeavour.
It'll be as a sacrifice. Ah'll pay you, dear Lord.
Whatever steps first from out ma front door.'

Well y'all see what stepped out. You'll say, 'What a fool!'
Did he not think and remember his daughter?
Sure he did for them Ammonites in unequal duel
But to bargain with fate? That's a fool of first water.
And as sure as ya knew it his daughter came out:
She was dancin' an' laughin' on hearing the news
How her father old Jephthah had put them to rout
Those Ammonite heathen. But his face gave some clues:
And his clothes torn in shreds showed his harror within.
But she, to soften his grief and his sin:
Said 'I'll be a nun for a month, no, two.
As yo' swore to yo' God what you would do, do!'
With her maidens she stayed up high on a hill
Till the months were done: down she came and was killed.

So think of the good ol' line: 'Beware!
Yo bargains will haunt yo 'less yo take best care!

What Joshua Fit

They marched round the walls in those distant days
And we know not for sure if the tale be true
But its grandeur lives on in the minds of today
For imagine the scene in that far-off time
Great walls metres thick and towers of stone
And the sun beating down on the Israelite heads –
A vast vanguard and trumpeters next –
Seven rams' horns blaring, beating those walls
Till the echoes rebounded and shook hearts within,
While next in the column on shoulders of priests
The mystical Ark of God's precious laws
Borne as much as a weapon as sword or spear

For the citizens knew of the power within
And had heard how the Jordan had stopped in its flow
How twelve Israelite tribes each bearing a stone
Crossed the river dry-foot as, in Moses' time,
They had crossed the Red Sea, which had swallowed their
                                                    foes.
And behind the bearers of God's precious laws
Thirty thousand marched proud beneath Joshua's eye.

For all the long day the watchers within
Heard the tramp of their feet and the clang of their shields,

Saw the glint of bright shields and the gleaming of spears
The helmets of brass and the armour of bronze
While the heat rose more fiery till evening grew dim
And the furnace of fear burned ever more fierce
In the heart of each woman, each man and each child.

Relentlessly marching for six days they strode
All knowing the climax the Lord had forewarned:
On day seven they marched seven times round the walls
Till, as a signal, great Joshua raised
With triumphant arm his spear to the sky
And all as one shouted and shattered the stones
And earth felt the thunder as granite and rock
Split their bindings, their mortar, their strength, tower by
                                                    tower
And the city was ground into choking dust.

But if not a word of the story is true
Perhaps as an image its message may stand
That the power of faith in the power of God,
If the power of God and his force is invoked,
Rends all to dust that impedes His Love
Or hinders the sweep of the march of Truth
When the bastions of evil dare stand in its path.

Three Act Play

(See I Samuel 17: 31-40)

Sheep graze, the sun climbs slow,
Silence is the day's essence, a backcloth
So unblemished that ants' footsteps violate.

A youth lies languishing but with ears alert.
So pure the silence it exaggerates all sounds.
He takes his instrument. At each touch notes
Echo in the hills like symphonies.

Hours pass, heat and light begin to fade.
Stones at his side he watches the bear
Sniffing in the shadows of a rock.
Long practised he feels one, smooth as an egg.
It nestles in the woven cup.
He waits,
Curling the leather strip around his hand.

The bear stiffens lifting his nose to the air
Sheep sleep upwind. Jewelled stars
Observe the swift trajectory
As the science of velocity and mass
Triple and triple till it strikes
Precisely home.

A month has passed since a like stone
Did its work.
The night grows cold.
A lion skin he slings across his shoulders.

These were the first two acts.
A finale awaits.

Theft

Uriah speaks...

'You, Joab, agent of that lecherous king
That thief, that coward, you have saved your skin.
You, fawner in the court of Jesse's son,
His vaunted general, have now withdrawn,
And knowingly have left me here for death.
Beneath these bitter walls, these foemen's towers,
Where now my life ebbs with my blood away.
Not only mine but blood of seventeen,
All noble men-at-arms of Judah's line,
Are sped to Sheol by your treachery.

Oh do not think I do not know your heart
Nor the king's heart. Dark as sin it lies.
And do not think I heard not of his lust.
His servant told me he had told the king
That Bathsheba, my Bathsheba, my queen,
Had with her beauty turned his raging fire
Of blind desire into that fire I felt
When first I glimpsed her in my spring of life.

He bade me, after our first fighting days,
After his lustful taste of Bathsheba,
To visit home. I knew his mind, I knew
The meaning of his words, "Go, wash your feet."
And so I stayed at court. I would not sleep

But near his door. I knew his mind, I knew.
He thought, if any child would spring from her
With me at home, a soldier, home on leave,
It would not then be deemed a child of his.

And I saw, Joab, next I saw that seal
That royal seal, upon those secret lines,
That, slyly, slyly, warranted my death.
"Set him before the place where hottest swords
May likeliest bring him death!" Now here I lie
And by my last breath he will gain his life
His life of endless joy in Bathsheba
Who was my life. And yet, if God be just,
Long days of misery may follow soon.'

These were Uriah's bitter dying words.
In Joab's shameful arms he lay and died.
And Joab bore him from the field of blood
And buried him, two loyalties in his breast
Contending equally with brands of fire.

*   *   *   *

Joab speaks...

'I, Joab, Judah's general-in-chief,
Make war, kill enemies and serve my king.
I deem which policies will serve. My loyalty
Is first unto myself. I test the winds
I seek the winners and my sole allies
Are what my steely will exonerates
Above all sentiment or foolish trusts.

My judgement has not failed. King David's will
Is my will, for I know a man who wins.
My master's mind I know and what he wills
Whether for what God deems be good
Or what the devil claims is rightly wrong
I execute. And I knew well his lust
Would not be baulked by piping principle.

I knew Uriah as a warrior
A man unparalleled in arts of war
I knew his value to my King's armies.
But, weighing craftily the loss and gain,
My interest was clearly for the king.
For failing of his will my own descent
Into the black pit he reserved for me
If I failed him. My path was clear: to kill.
Let others mourn the loss of such a man.

Besides, I will not hide the truth: I envied him
For he was little loath to boast his joy
In amorous delight with Bathsheba.

When I received that letter from the king,
I could not hide a slow smirk spreading then
With secret joy: into my grasp had come,
Unbidden, that forbidden fruit, that means
To be the lawful executioner
Of him who, otherwise, might on some day
Be my usurper, my dark nemesis.
I had my orders, saw my duty clear.'

*   *   *   *

Bathsheba speaks…

'In future times I know not whether men
Will call me evil whore or innocent.
I know not whether beauty is my curse
Or whether God has drawn my course of life
Into a shape to please His fitful mind
Unknowable, capricious or divine.
But with the beauty I possess I know
That with it I can shape men in one mould.

That day I bathed, so sultry, so becalmed,
And such a fever running in my veins!
For dutifully, after the seven day law
Leviticus enjoins upon us wives,
I bathed outside where, in the courtyard shade,
So cooling, where the doves make yearning moan,
And in the shadows of the palace walls,
I stretched and dropped by chance my silken robe.

Few minutes passed. I stretched again.
Whereat a servant girl came blushingly
And told her tale: that from the king
Enquiries had been made: was I a maid
Or wife? And if a maid to come forthwith
Into the palace where King David dwelt.

It was a sad truth, I will not deny
That must be told. That I was married then

To Uri, man of war, a man of strength,
'A mighty man of valor' — as was said
Also of him whose lofty head was sliced
Clean off by David, now a king of power,
—I mean Goliath brutish Philistine.
For had I been a maid, into the house
I doubtless would have entered, there to be
Another of the king's close concubines.

Perhaps I felt a pang, knowing the king
To be a man whose mighty deeds
Whether defeating lion, bear or wolf
Had thrilled us when we were but foolish maids.

But in a moment more, despite my state,
More messengers appeared and bore me off
Into the palace. 'Lie with me,' he said.
"But Sire, I am no maid." I cried, yet knew
That was no bar to stem his lust – or mine.
And feverishly we lay a long time there
Within the palace while the evening light
Deepened and drew us with love's secret flame.

And soon at home I knew what stirred within.
The die was cast. Disgrace and death were mine
When my Uriah would return from war.'

*   *   *   *

David speaks…

'That day I slept, that hot day when I rose
After the shadows crept across the floor
That day when I, like Adam, tasted life
Or was it death? I only know that I
Was king no longer of untainted land.
For death and sorrow and repentance deep
Became my new life after Bathsheba.
All that remained to me was death and war.
Yet on that day I swear that I
Was no more than a servant or a slave.

Upon the rooftop after long repose,
I walked and ambled in the cooling breeze
Until the sharpest stab of beauty's sting
Inducted strongest fever to my soul.
We lay in heaven's counterfeit that day
Until the evening's fading light begat
The long decline and downward spiralling.
No logic, no necessity, no bar
No upward way could turn me from the path.

I now became a minister of death.
My first essay was to find subterfuge
Uriah I invited to take leave:
He need not go to Rabbah where the siege
Was in full swing, but, 'Go on home, my friend,'

I craftily but vainly urged. 'Go, take
Your rest – take in your arms your wife.
Embrace her after such brave toils of war,
You've earned the right.' But he, with darkened eyes
Suspiciously refused. 'How take my rest,'
He nobly spoke, 'when brave men lie awake
On watch upon the baleful battlefield
While I in comfort with my dearest wife
Upon a soft bed lie at peace and rest?'
And in the morning, from my adjutant,
I learned that he had lain beside my door.
And so for many more nights he did so.

I tried again, another subterfuge —
Invited him to dine and plied him well
With wine and wassail till his dark eyes swam
Unsoberly. Yet still he cried: 'My friend,
The general, my comrade, Jo, and all
The armies of your lordship's mighty realm
Together with the sacred tented ark,
Lie all exposed to spear and sword and death.
No, my great lord, I cannot homeward go
And dine and feed and share my bed of love.'

My shame now deepened, knowing what I planned
Yet utterly unable to desist
Or fetter my desire for Bathsheba.

My final shame, now that the way was blocked
To my unbridled lust, was to engage
My nephew, Joab, my chief general.
I sent him letters making clear the plan
To set huge odds against Uriah's life
By placing him where death stalked certainly.

All came to pass and briefly all seemed well.
I hid my guilt beneath the cloak of love,
Took Bathsheba to wife and my new queen.
But it was soon my shame was new exposed:
Nathan, the prophet, wise and kind and good,
Shirked nothing of the truth, dared to my face
To utter all my sin and told this tale:
"A rich man stole a poor man's only lamb.
Though he had flocks and herds beyond enough,
He was too cruel to take from his own flocks
A single beast to entertain one man,
A traveller who passed by on a day."

I rose in wrath to hear this cruelty
Till Nathan with an old man's piercing eye
Declared the thief was King, the lamb was queen
For it was I, I was the thief who stole
I was the murderer, and for this crime
The prophet warned me that for all my power
My sin would hence besiege me with great grief.

This prophecy in after days was truth:
My son by Bathsheba lived but few years
I made a deep confession before God
Who heard my prayer and saved me from the pit;
But all remaining years saw deaths and strife
And war and my own family, my son,
My dearest son, my dearest Absalom
Rose up in treachery to claim my crown
Till fleeing through a wood to 'scape my wrath
A forked branch caught and held him by the neck
And he was butchered by my angry men.

Yet God is merciful, for Bathsheba
Bore yet a son who yet I hope will live
Beyond my fame and build that prayer in stone —
The temple that I longed myself to build
For my atonement for my evil crimes.

Now to my knees I fall again in prayer
For Solomon, for wisdom, mercy, rest…

A Dance

The girl swayed subtly sinuously, fine,
Before the drunken king engulphed in wine
Her gossamer enticements softly floated down –
Seven it's said – so slowly to the ground
The king's eyes all but burst out from his bulging head.
'Tell me' he whispered, 'what you wish', he said,
'For half my kingdom you may ask and on my oath
It shall be given – let these guests know it, by my troth.'
Salome, nearly naked, smiled and smiled
And knew her act had perfectly beguiled
The king, besotted with her youthful flesh,
And from Herodias, her mother, watchful, fresh
From her angered musing of the Baptist's word
Asked now what prize to seek and had she heard
That half his kingdom she could claim – 'The head'
Her mother snarled, not listening more, and said,
'Of that insulting prophet John. Bring it on a dish
So it can grace this feast. That is my wish.'
For in her mind his rankling words resounded still
That she unlawfully had wed; so to fulfil
Her vengeful brain, she'd planned the feast
So ill content only to think the saint deceased
Would end her bitterness.

Salome, trembling with this answer, came
Back to Herod. He saddened with self-blame
(For even he knew John a greater man than he)
Could not untie his own knot but agree
And sent a minion to the prison cell
There to behead the saint. So it befell
That into this gross feast upon a plate
The bloodied head of John, such evil freight
From such a saintly man, filled up the room
With horror: such a death foredoomed

About the Author

Robin Barton

Robin spent most of his earlier life as an English teacher at Claremont School Near Esher, Surrey.

He enjoyed running in his earlier days, including the London Marathon and two half marathons near Newcastle.

He enjoys classical music and especially watching birds.

He was educated at Peter Symonds College at Winchester and Manchester Universty (BA) and studies Christian Science.

About the Illustrator and Compiler

Melissa Muldoon

Melissa is an artist, sculptor and illustrator. Inspired hugely by nature and our beautiful planet, obsessed with making the world a lovelier place and bringing imagination to life.

Melissa always has numerous projects on the go at any one time, she illustrates books, runs children's art workshops, builds sculptures (mostly out of pre-loved materials) for community projects and private commissions, and works in graphic/logo design in her 'spare' time.

Previous illustrated books include
The Mouse's House, Mouse's Best Day Ever,
Mouse And The Storm, T-Rex to Chicken,
Moonlight in the Garden, Inside The Broom Cupboard,
The Pug in the Helmet and The Hippopotamermaid. Still in the pipeline are numerous mindful books, illustrated works for poetry and many more exciting projects!

Melissa is committed to helping everyone get their book into print.

Visit www.melissamuldoon.co.uk for more information.

Printed in Great Britain
by Amazon